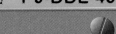

Bob the Builder™

Dizzy and Muck Work It Out

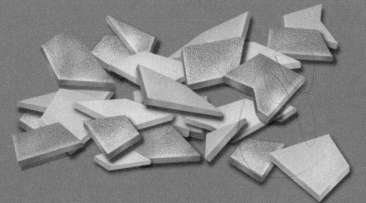

adapted by
Annie Auerbach

based on the script by
Diane Redmond

illustrated by
Joe and Terri Chicko

SCHOLASTIC INC.

New York Toronto London Auckland Sydney
Mexico City New Delhi Hong Kong Buenos Aires

Based upon the television series *Bob the Builder*™ created by HIT Entertainment PLC and Keith Chapman, with thanks to HOT Animation, as seen on Nick Jr.®

No part of this publication may be reproduced in whole or in part, or stored in a retrieval system, or transmitted in any form or by any means, electronic, mechanical, photocopying, recording, or otherwise, without written permission of the publisher. For information regarding permission, write to Simon Spotlight, an imprint of Simon & Schuster Children's Publishing Division, 1230 Avenue of the Americas, New York, NY 10020.

ISBN 0-439-40571-8

12 11 10 9 8 7 6 5 4 3 2 1   2 3 4 5 6 7/0

Printed in the U.S.A.

First Scholastic printing, September 2002

Bob and Wendy had just finished plastering Mrs. Broadbent's wall.

"The plaster's drying nicely," Bob said. "We should be able to paint it this afternoon."

"Oh, good," said Wendy. "I need to run over to Mrs. Potts's house. She's asked me to lay a new path in her garden."

Wendy hurried back to the building yard to get the team. Muck, Roley, and Dizzy were loaded up and ready to go.

"Can we pave it?" Wendy asked.
"YES, WE CAN!" the team shouted excitedly.

When they got there, Wendy asked Mrs. Potts where she would like the new path in her garden to go.

Mrs. Potts wasn't sure. "I want it to go near my statues. . . ."

"Which are your favorites?" asked Wendy.

"Oh, the Greek god and Cheeky Charlie!" Mrs. Potts told Wendy proudly.

"Then the new path should definitely go near those two!" replied
Wendy.

"Wonderful!" Mrs. Potts cried. "Just be extra careful of Cheeky Charlie,
and make sure you don't flatten my flower beds."

"Don't worry, we'll take care of everything," Wendy reassured her.

Mrs. Potts still seemed unsure, but she had to go to the store to pick up
some groceries, so she left.

The team went to work.

Just then Wendy's cell phone rang. "Hi, Bob! . . . The plaster's dried? . . . Okay, I'll get Roley to give me a lift. See you soon."

Wendy went back outside
and instructed Muck and Dizzy
to lay the paving stones on
the path while she was gone.

"You're going to leave Muck and Dizzy on their own?" Roley asked as they drove back to Mrs. Broadbent's house.

"Just for a little while," replied Wendy.

"Uh-oh," Roley said quietly. He knew what trouble Muck and Dizzy could get into together.

"Is everything all right in Mrs. Potts's garden?" Bob asked Wendy.

"Yes," replied Wendy. "I left Muck and Dizzy in charge of laying the paving stones."

Bob was surprised. "Do you think it's a good idea to leave those two alone? You know how they get into trouble sometimes."

"They'll be fine," Wendy reassured him.

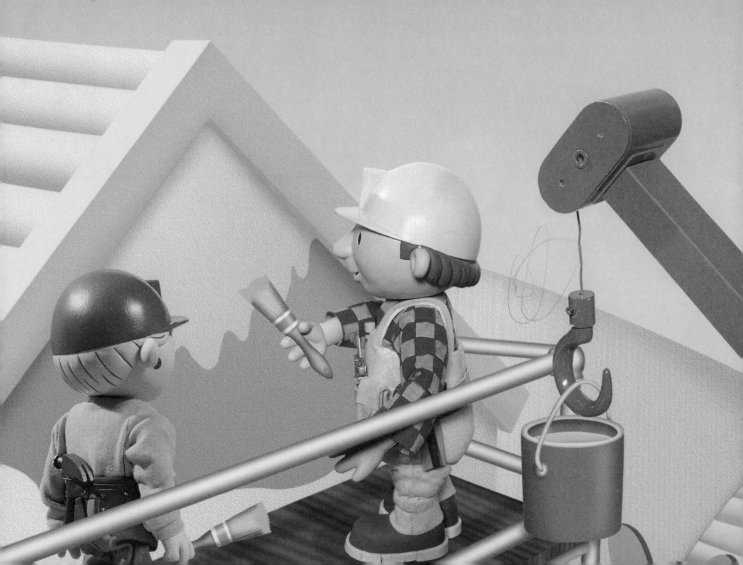

But Muck and Dizzy *weren't* fine.

"Okay, let's go, Muck!" Dizzy said in a bossy voice.

"Hey, Wendy said for us to do this *together!*" Muck replied, rumbling toward Dizzy.

"Watch out for Cheeky Charlie!"
Dizzy shouted.

Muck swerved to avoid hitting
Cheeky Charlie, and the paving
stones flew into the air . . .

. . . and broke into pieces on the ground!
  "Oh, no!" Muck cried. "The paving stones!"
  "And look at Cheeky Charlie!" added Dizzy.
  The statue's nose was chipped!

Back at Mrs. Broadbent's house, Bob was still worried about Muck and Dizzy.

"Maybe I'd better check to see how things are going at Mrs. Potts's garden," Wendy suggested.

"Good idea!" Bob said, relieved.

"Oh, no!" Wendy cried when she arrived. "Now what are we going to do?"
"I have an idea!" said Dizzy. "We can use the broken stones to make a path."
"Crazy paving!" Wendy exclaimed.
"You mean crazy *Dizzy*." Muck laughed.

"No, crazy paving is when you make a path out of broken paving stones," Wendy explained.

"Hee, hee, it's Dizzy's crazy paving!" Muck said.

"Yippee!" cheered Dizzy. "Let's get to work!"

Working together, Muck and Dizzy got the job done.
"Hey, it looks great!" Muck exclaimed. "You're really clever, Dizzy!"
"Thanks, Muck," replied Dizzy. "But I couldn't have done it without you!"

When Bob finished painting Mrs. Broadbent's wall, he decided to see
how Mrs. Potts's garden path was coming along.

"Hi, Bob," said Mrs. Potts, who was just coming home from the store.
"What perfect timing! Let's go see my new garden path together!"

Bob and Mrs. Potts couldn't believe their eyes.
"You've made crazy paving!" Bob exclaimed. "Good job, everyone!"
Mrs. Potts clapped her hands with excitement. "It's so pretty!"

"Whose idea was it to use those little pieces of stone?" Mrs. Potts asked.
"It was *our* idea!" Muck and Dizzy said together. Then they looked at
Wendy.

"Actually, we had an accident and we broke the paving stones," Muck confessed. "We're sorry!"

"That's okay," said Mrs. Potts. Then she looked at her new path and smiled warmly. "I think your accident made a beautiful surprise! And I always thought Cheeky Charlie's nose was too big anyway!"

"That's our team," said Wendy with a smile. "We're always coming up with *smashing* ideas!"